Dedicated to all of the animals who need a home and thanks to those who rescue and adopt them

A Home for Hugo

Written and Illustrated by Leigh Nisonson

© 2021 Leigh Nisonson

ISBN 978-1-09837-315-3

A Home for Hugo

Written and Illustrated by Leigh Nisonson

My name is **Hugo**.
Though I did not always have the
name Hugo.
In fact, I did not have a name at all.
I did not have a home either.

My journey is sad but has a happy ending.
This is the story of my wanderings
and quest for a home.
Segun dicen...

My tale begins in Quito, the capital city of Ecuador, South America. It is a beautiful city elevated high above the sea, nestled snuggly within the Pinchincha volcanoes and the Guayllabamba River. The people who live in Quito are called Quitans.

There are also many dogs living in Quito, but sadly a lot of them are street dogs. They do not have a home or family to care for them. They beg for food and find kindness from strangers wherever they can.

Unfortunately, not everyone is nice to street dogs. Some people are afraid of them, and others do not like them around begging for food. They chase them away with brooms and throw pebbles at them. Some **malo** people take puppies and sell them to a make a quick **sucre**.

But I digress. My real odyssey begins when my mother gave birth to a litter of ten puppies. It was a cool November day as the clouds passed over the Quitan volcanoes, and 5 girls and 5 boys were born. I was the last to arrive. She loved all of her babies, but she spoiled me as the youngest of a mother's babies is often spoiled.

My mother always made sure that I was the first to drink. She pushed the bigger pups away until my pink belly puffed out like a blow-fish, full of **leche**. As I drifted off to sleep, my mother lapped clean my wrinkle-mouth and big floppy brown ears.

My family lived on the streets. But my mother took such good care of us, that I did not even realize I was a street dog.

My mother told us, "When you are with your family, you have a **casa**. Your family is your **casa**. Even though we do not have an actual **casa**, sticking together as a family is our **casa** and that gives us strength."

At nighttime, when the Quitan winds blew fiercely and the volcanoes rumbled and shook the Quitan earth, my mother saved the soft cushion between her chin and neck for me. Once I was asleep, she squeezed her neck down to give me extra warmth.

As the days passed, and her babies grew, my mother told us, "you will become strong and big, and, one day, you will have your own puppies to look after. Over time, you will learn how to fend for yourself. I will not always be here, but — don't be sad — when that time comes, I know that you will be strong, as I will teach you to be."
Each day I tried to become an adult, just like my mother. Life was **bueno**.

One night when my sisters and brothers had already fallen asleep, I looked up at the big **luna** reflecting in my mother's eyes. She told me, "Life is not easy on the street. Not everyone is lucky enough to have a home. But there are ways, and you will find them. Take advantage of every opportunity that comes. Life is easier in a home, with someone special."

"But you are special to me, mommy. Why would I need a home when I have everything I want right here?"

"Little Hugo, you will see, one day, there will be someone as special as me. And a home is the most special thing I could ever wish for you. I know you will find one."

As we got older, my mother brought us to the market to find scraps for dinner. It was very busy. People rushed back and forth carrying baskets of goodies. My mother warned us to stay close so we would not lose her.

One day at the market, I caught wind of the sweet aroma of a **fritada** filled with corn, cheese, potatoes and plantains. I had not eaten in days, and the sweet smell was over-powering. Ahh, I thought, if only my mother could just snag one **fritada** and we could all share the treat. One **fritada** would leave me feeling full for days.

As I dreamed about sinking my tiny baby teeth into a **fritada**, I suddenly realized .... My mother was nowhere nearby. Where was my mother? Where were my siblings? I felt cold and alone, and the tears welled up in my eyes. Maybe if I just trotted along in the same direction I would find her.

I trotted. I ran. I sprinted in circles around the food stands. I looked as far as my little puppy eyes could see. I ran as far as my little tired puppy paws would go. Still no sign of my mother. No siblings. All alone. Utterly and totally alone.
I cried, using the sounds I had used to let my mother know I was hungry, thirsty, cold and scared. I was all of these things right now, but most of all I just missed my mother.

A long and lonely night passed. When the **sol** finally rose, I recalled a time when I loved to watch the orange rays grow deeper hues as I cuddled with my mother. Now, the **sol** did not bring me joy and I was terrified to meet the coming day.

After my first night alone, an even longer day passed. People shooed me away. No one wanted me around. I tried to put on a brave face.

I walked onto a quiet street and spotted some children – **los muchachos** and **las muchachas** – playing in a **huerta**. My desperate thoughts were swept away by the sweet happy voices and the colorful **flores**. My heart skipped a beat with joy when the smallest **muchacha** swept me into her arms. I knew she would protect me while I looked for my mommy.

The girl's name was Risa, which means laughter in Spanish. Risa opened the **huerta** gate and carried me into her house.

"Mamma, look at the cute puppy I found – he wandered into our **huerta** from the street and he needs a home."

"Risa, no..."
But she stopped mid-sentence as her icy glare was warmed by my golden puppy eyes. This was my chance, I thought.

"Oh, he is so little ... well, don't tell your father. Keep him in the **huerta**."

For the next few months, I lived blissfully in Risa's **huerta**. Delicious new smells at every turn. And plenty of time to dream. I would walk along the roses trailing the walls, smelling each bud, and delicately sampling the dew drops on each leaf, careful not to scrape my nose on the thorns.

In the afternoons, Risa's friends would come to play. Sometimes I lay belly-up in the grass watching the butterflies while **las muchachas** gave me tummy rubs. Other times, I sprinted in circles around the **flores**, chasing the children in a game of tag. I would then drift off to sleep as the **sol** set. Life was **bueno** again.

Risa would bring a bowl of
caliente leche and treats
for breakfast.

She scooped me up as I sipped
leche and nibbled pieces of
cookie out of her palm.

It went on like this
for a few months ...
until I began
to grow ...

After all the **leche**, cookies, and long naps in the **huerta**, I was now twice the size as when I first arrived.

Risa could no longer pick me up. I was not a puppy anymore. And my time in the **huerta** was coming to an end.

After dinner that night, Risa's father said,
"that dog is getting too big, you cannot keep him any longer."

Risa cried but she had to obey her father's order. She gave me my
goodnight **beso**. I whimpered because I tasted the salty tears on her
face and I had never seen Risa, who was so full of laughter, crying.
"I'm sorry but **vamos**" she sobbed.
My whimpers turned to cries. Once again, I had no home.
Once again, I was just a street dog.

The next few weeks passed very slowly.
As I wandered around Quito, people pushed me away yelling,
"Vamos!"
At night, I hid under a bridge, trying to disappear into the darkness.
I longed for a tender hug and a goodnight **beso** from Risa.

And, mostly, I ached for the companionship of **los muchachos**
and **las muchachas**. On the streets I was invisible; and if I was
noticed, I was not wanted.

Eventually my wandering brought me to a grocery store,
where a dog was lying outside. Was this doggie a friend or foe?
Her tired eyes met my piercing stare. **Amiga.**
She stayed outside the store, because the shop owner's wife would
throw out food. The food was spoiled, but she needed to feed her
puppies growing in her belly. I stuck by her like glue. She was my
temporary mamma. She was my Risa. She was my best **amiga**.
Did she have a name? I called her Ami.

One day, the shop owner found me blocking the entrance.
"I cannot have this street dog interfering with my business."
He said that I needed to leave his store or... **un problema**.

Word spread from the shop owner to the shoppers, but no one
wanted me. What was another street dog without a home?
It was a common occurrence in Quito.
"VAMOS" the shop owner said.

I said farewell to Ami and walked down the
highway, away from the store.
Where would I go now?
Where was my home?
As I rounded a corner,
I collided nose-first with a big camera lens.
Acaso!

I stumbled backwards.
Looking up I saw the bright shining **sol** and a blurry
figure behind a camera.
Who was this person I had collided with in the street?
All of a sudden the camera flashed,

"Click!"
"Whrrr!"

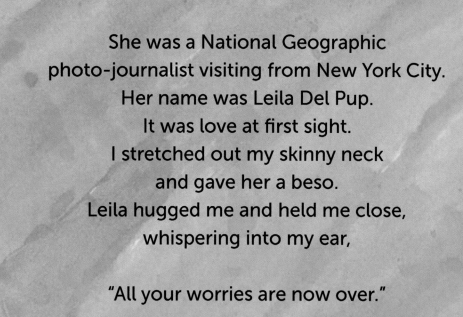

She was a National Geographic
photo-journalist visiting from New York City.
Her name was Leila Del Pup.
It was love at first sight.
I stretched out my skinny neck
and gave her a beso.
Leila hugged me and held me close,
whispering into my ear,

"All your worries are now over."

Leila gave me fresh water and warm gooey cookies.
For the first time in a while, my tummy felt full.
But, what else did I need?
A **bano**. After living on the street, I was very smelly.
Leila plopped me in a tub filled with warm water, soap-suds,
and bubbles.

Leila even brushed my tiny baby teeth until they gleamed and glistened sparkly white, like candy chicklets from the grocery store.

When Leila was finished, she used a fluffy **toalla de bano** to wipe me dry and gave me a goodnight **beso**. That night, I slept very well, dreaming of **flores** and my angel, Leila.

The next day, my picture and story hit the National Geographic website. Leila showed me the article on her laptop, explaining her mission to help street dogs all over the world find homes.

Leila's story documented the stray dogs in Quito, and after Quito, Leila planned to visit other countries, bringing international attention to the difficult lives of street dogs, and hopefully finding a solution.

Leila explained to me that, if I wanted, she would adopt me and I could go to New York City to live with her. "Once you are adopted, you get to live with one family forever. They will love you and take care of you; you are a part of their family — they are your family. Hugo, I want you to be part of my family. Do you want that too?"

Without hesitation I nodded yes and jumped on Leila giving her a big **beso**. I finally had a home.

Leila made travel arrangements and began to prepare me for
life in a home. It was time for some training.
Leila taught me how to "sit" and "stay."
She bought me a plane **boleto** to New York City, and took me to get a
passport and a suitcase. I chose a red suitcase, and got my passport
picture taken. "Cheese!"

I packed my suitcase. Passport, plane **boleto** — check. I was ready to go!
As Leila drove me to the airport, I looked out the window and watched
as the city of Quito grew smaller and smaller behind me.

At the airport, I climbed a steep flight of stairs
and boarded the airplane.

I was leaving Ecuador to embark on my new life
but my lost family was still heavy in my heart.

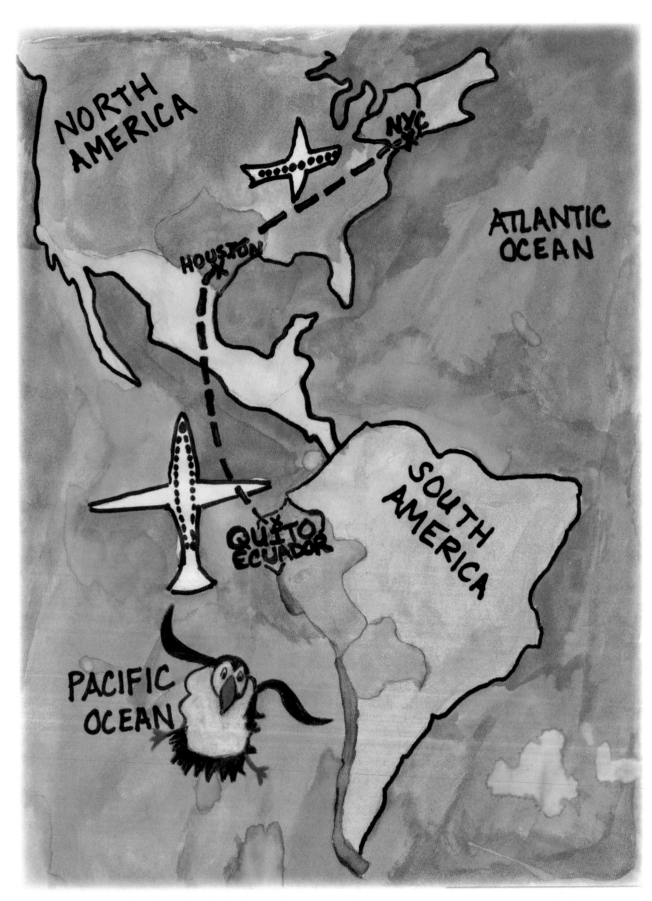

My journey from Quito to New York City lasted
twenty-three hours, almost one full day.

I travelled by plane....

Until I finally reached HOME. Our **casa** is in the West Village.

New York City is so beautiful, and my home is so comfortable.
I love sitting on a park bench with Leila watching the **sol** set behind the
skyscrapers and walking along the Hudson River Park
promenade as the boats sail into the marina.

I enjoy seeing squirrels run up the trees and ducks
swimming with the koi fish in the pond.
New York City is magical.

Even my friend, Puffin, has found a home.

I have finally found my home.
A home for Hugo.
And now that I am settled,
I think I will search for my mother, sisters
and brothers....

THE END.........
until my next adventure!

Spanish to English Glossary

Segun dicen	As the story goes
Malo	Evil
Sucre	Dollar
Leche	Milk
Casa	Home
Bueno	Good
Luna	Moon
Fritada	Dish of fried fish
Sol	Sun
Los muchachos	The boys
Las muchachas	The girls
Huerta	Garden
Flores	Flowers
Caliente	Warm
Beso	Kiss
Amiga	Friend
Un problema	A problem
Vamos!	Let's go!
Acaso	By chance, accident
Bano	Bath
Toalla de bano	Bath towel
Boleto	Ticket